One Mole
Digging A Hole

For Mhairi
and Eilidh
J.D.

For Neil, gardener
extraordinaire
N.S.

First published 2008 by Macmillan Children's Books
This edition published 2010 by Macmillan Children's Books
a division of Macmillan Publishers Limited
20 New Wharf Road, London N1 9RR
Basingstoke and Oxford
Associated companies throughout the world
www.panmacmillan.com

ISBN: 978-0-330-53251-8

5 7 9 8 6 4

A CIP catalogue record for this book is available from the British Library.

Printed in China

One Mole Digging A Hole

Written by

Julia Donaldson

Illustrated by

Nick Sharratt

MACMILLAN CHILDREN'S BOOKS

One mole

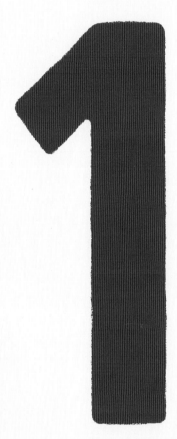

1

digging a hole

Two snakes

with garden rakes

Three bears

3

picking pears

Four foxes

filling boxes

Five storks

with garden forks

Six parrots

pulling up carrots

Seven frogs

7

chopping logs

Eight crows

8

with a garden hose

Nine doves

9

in gardening gloves

Ten bees

10

pruning trees

EVERYONE enjoying the sun!